Other Yearling Books You Will Enjoy

TOYS GO OUT, *Emily Jenkins*

MY ONE HUNDRED ADVENTURES, *Polly Horvath*

NORTHWARD TO THE MOON, *Polly Horvath*

MOXY MAXWELL DOES NOT
LOVE *STUART LITTLE*, *Peggy Gifford*

PICTURES OF HOLLIS WOODS, *Patricia Reilly Giff*

May B.

A Novel

by Caroline Starr Rose

A YEARLING BOOK

Text copyright © 2012 by Caroline Starr Rose
Cover art copyright © 2012 by Christopher Silas Neal

The Library of Congress has cataloged the hardcover edition
of this work as follows:
Rose, Caroline Starr.
May B. : a novel-in-verse / by Caroline Starr Rose.—1st ed.
p. cm.
Summary: When a failed wheat crop nearly bankrupts the Betterly
family, Pa pulls twelve-year-old May from school and hires
her out to a couple new to the Kansas frontier.
ISBN 978-1-58246-393-3 (hardcover) — ISBN 978-1-58246-412-1
(gibraltar library binding) — ISBN 978-1-58246-437-4 (ebook)
[1. Novels in verse. 2. Frontier and pioneer life—Kansas—Fiction.
3. Kansas—History—19th century—Fiction.] I. Title.
PZ7.5.R67May 2011
[Fic]—dc22
2010033222
ISBN 978-0-385-37414-9 (pbk.)

Printed in the United States of America
10 9 8 7 6

First Yearling Edition 2014

In loving memory of my grandmother,
Gene Starr Craig

For my students in New Mexico, Florida, Virginia, and
Louisiana: There are a few of you whose needs I didn't
fully understand and others I could have done better by.
This story is for you.

Part One

I won't go.

"It's for the best," Ma says,
yanking to braid my hair,
trying to make something of what's left.

Ma and Pa want me to leave
and live with strangers.

I won't go.

"It's for the best,
you packing up and moving
to the Oblingers' soddy."
Ma's brush tugs.
My eyes sting.

For the best,
like when the Wright baby died,
not three weeks old—
one less child to clothe.

After all,
I cook some,
collect fuel,
mend,
tote water,
hoe,
wash,
pretty braid or not.

Why not Hiram? I think,
but I already know:
boys are necessary.

"You'll bring in some extra money," Ma says.

"We'll get you home by Christmas."
A wisp of hair escapes her grasp,
encircling my cheek.

For the best,
one less child to clothe.

Before Ma ties my ribbon,
I push outside and run.
My feet pound out
I won't go
I won't go
I won't go.

My braid spills loose.
The short pieces hang about one ear.
Hiram—
the hunk of hair he cut
because I dared him to.
He got his lashing
like we knew he would,
his smile full of pride.
Why didn't he cut it all?
Then maybe,
like Samson in the Bible,
I'd be useless too.

I stop when home is nothing more
than a mound on the windswept plain.
Like a prairie hen I settle down
until I can't be seen,
breathing comfort from grass and soil.
I listen for silence,
but there's no room for it.
My mind's too full.
Ma and Pa want me to leave
and live with strangers.

Around my finger
I twist a blade of grass.
It's what I've always wanted,
to contribute,
but not this way.
If I leave,
schooling is as good as finished.
Come Christmas I'll be home
but even farther
behind.

In three more years
I'll be old enough.
In three more years

maybe
I'll be able to teach.

I grab a fistful of shorn hair.
I *am* no better than Samson
once that Delilah cut his hair,
once his strength was gone.
Powerless.
Defeated.

Mavis Elizabeth Betterly
May Betts
May B.

Somehow Hiram spots me.
"What're you hiding for?" he asks.
I stand up and punch him on the arm,
for cutting my hair,
for being a boy,
for reading strong,
easy as you please.
I punch him again.

Hiram rubs his shoulder,
then hooks his arm through mine.
"Ma asked me to fetch you.
Suppertime."

Our soddy's dark and smells like the prairie
with its freshness stolen away.
Ma's laid the table;
Pa's boots are near the door.

I tuck my hair behind my ears
and sit down with Hiram.
"Ma told you?" Pa asks
straight after grace.
"Better pack tonight."

I nod,
stare down at the chicken fixings
(no everyday salt pork tonight).
Ma's even set out tinned peaches.

"The homestead's fifteen miles west of here,"
   Pa says.
"The bride's not settled,
got here after Oblinger built his soddy."
Pa looks at me.
"She's missing home."

Won't I miss home?
Ma touches my hand.

"It's just till Christmas, May."

I push away,
my peaches left untouched.

Once the table's cleared and Hiram's out with
 Pa,
Ma opens her hope chest.
She unfolds her finest pillowcase
and slips my Sunday dress inside.
She adds her old calico,
worn a yellow-brown,
and a chemise
made by her own ma.

"You'll need some shoes."
Ma pulls out boots I rarely see,
dainty and ladylike.
I'm to leave Hiram's old pair for her.

Three dresses,
counting my work dress.
Ma's chemise,
along with my own.
Two sets of stockings.
Two pairs of bloomers.
Two aprons.
My coat.
Woolen mittens.
New shoes.

I pull the crate from under my bed,
taking my reader and my slate.

Ma sighs. "Ain't no way you'll keep up
with the rest."
"I know," I say.

I catch what's not said:
it's foolishness to keep pretending.
What sort of teacher can't read out lessons?

Maybe May B. can
Maybe May B. can't

I remember when we first came
what Pa used to say.
"Hiram and you are as young as Kansas.
As fresh to life
as the Prairie State."

Those traveling weeks we watched the sky
from the wagon
or walking beside it,
hoping to be the first to spy
the distant place where
the ground and air connect.
This became our game,
Hiram's and mine,
and once on our land,
farther west than ever before,
we stood
on the gentle rise
where the coneflowers and wild mustard
    bloom.
Wind cutting my eyes,
I searched for
that place where land touches sky.

9

While Pa fetches the wagon in the early-
    morning black,
Hiram pulls me around back.
He doesn't need to tell me
we're going to the gentle rise
where wildflowers grow.

Hiram and I stand high
as the countryside allows.
Behind us,
there's the smallest hint of sun.

"Remember, May Betts,
it's just beyond."
Hiram points into the darkness,
like I might forget.
We haven't seen it yet,
but we know it's there.

Pa's taking me farther west,
toward sunset and rain,
farther from town than Hiram's ever been.

I hold out my hand.
"If I see it first,

you owe me your Christmas candy.
If you see it, I'll give you mine."
Hiram's fingers squeeze my hand. "Agreed."

"How do I know you'll be honest?" I say.
He squints at me.
"I wouldn't lie.
That takes the fun out of winning."

Hiram's better at races,
always grabs the extra biscuit.
Ma's first spring baby,
he beat me to living
by one short year.
And now,
for once,
I'll be ahead.

"Maybe I'll see it first," I say.
Hiram tags me
fast,
then starts to run home.
"Or maybe not!" he tosses back.

Our mare pulls,
the wagon sways,
the grass ripples.
Only I am holding back.

Pa's hunched over the reins.
I wonder when he'll speak his piece.
Since last night's supper he's been
silent.

I find myself inside the rhythm
of hoof
and wheel
and join this going forward,
but I am behind, still.

I play a game inside my head,
counting plum trees that dot a creek bed,
rabbits that scatter at the sound of wagon
   wheels,
clouds that skirt the sky.
For hours, that is all,
and grass,
always grass,
in different shades and textures
like the braids in a rag rug.

Miss Sanders told us that lines never end,
and numbers go on forever.
Here,
in short-grass country,
I understand infinity.

We stop just once to eat,
after the sun has reached its peak.
I watch a bird balance
on a blade of grass
bent low toward earth
to find a meal.
All creatures must work for their keep.

"I know schooling's what you want,
but with this spring's wheat . . ."
Pa shrugs.

"Will Hiram go back?"
I have to know.
He's thirteen now,
one of the oldest boys
still learning.

Pa's eyes meet mine.
"No," he says,
"I'll need his help around the place."
I shut my eyes,
catch Hiram's smile.
All term he's complained,
wanting to be a man and work the farm.

"You're helping out, May," Pa says.
I'm helping everyone
except myself.

I see the homestead first:
an awkward lump of earth,
a lazy curl of smoke above.
Beyond the soddy,
a barn carved into a hill.
Pa doesn't need to point but does.
"It's not as nice as what we've got.
Did most of his work alone.
Still plenty of time for improvements."

Pa cut our strips of sod.
He and Ma stacked them,
layer by layer,
grass side down,
using only a bit of precious wood to frame
our windows and door.

This soddy's small,
the earthen walls misshapen,
just one papered window.

I clutch my pillowcase.

Mr. Oblinger spies us,
waves,

steps inside his home.
Later,
when we're closer,
I catch the flaming red of Mrs. Oblinger's
    dress.
She stands in the doorway for a time,
facing us.
It's only when we approach
that she shuts herself inside.

I stay in the wagon,
watching Pa and Mr. Oblinger
inspect the garden,
point toward empty prairie.
Without hearing,
I know the talk
of plow,
of wheat,
of rain
and promise.

Hand passes to hand,
and Pa tucks money
inside his shirt pocket.

It's then he motions toward me.
I can't pretend not to see.

Pa gives my shoulders a gentle squeeze.
"This here's Mavis."
"May," I say.
"Glad to have you with us, May."
Mr. Oblinger shakes Pa's hand.
"You sure you don't want to stay?"
"No, thank you," Pa says.

"We need provisions from town.
I'll sleep there tonight."

Pa pulls me close,
the crisp money crackles
against my cheek.
My first wage.
"Till Christmas," he says.
"Do your best."

I nod.

But I know
my best isn't always good enough.

I don't wait until Pa's far
before I turn toward the door.
Watching him
would only stretch the distance.

Just a push swings the door open.
The air inside is heavy
with heat,
with darkness,
with something I can't name.

Mrs. Oblinger turns,
her skirts
swirl,
her eyes
study me like a lesson.
She's fancy and tall,
but I've caught it right away—
she's hardly older than I.

"This here's where you'll sleep."
She holds out her arm,
like showing me
a spot vast as the prairie.
Not a hint of privacy—

a dingy corner,
muslin pinned across the ceiling
stained brown
from rain that seeps through the sod.
I stand straight.
"Thank you, ma'am."

Mrs. Oblinger slices the air with one finger.
"Use this crate for your belongings."

She catches my glance at the ceiling,
the sagging cloth already filled with bits of
   soil.
I drop my chin,
study my shoes.

"You'll be no wetter than the rest of us," she
   says.

"Once you unpack,
you can start in on supper."
I wait for her to turn away,
so I might have one moment to myself.
Mrs. Oblinger doesn't budge.

From the pillowcase,
I pull Ma's calico.
My reader tumbles to the floor.
Mrs. Oblinger scoops it up,
opens the cover slowly,
touches the place I've written my name.
I rip it from her hands and hold it to my chest.

"What was that for?" she demands.
"It's mine," I say.
"Careful, young lady." She flings the words,
more girl than woman herself.

My apology spills out.
"I won't let my schoolwork interfere with
    chores."

Mrs. Oblinger's eyes meet mine.

"I was under the impression you
couldn't read a thing.
Once you unpack,
start in on supper."

I dump my belongings in a pile,
yank off Ma's fancy boots,
my toes more comfortable on the hard-packed
    earth.
My reader and slate I wrap in the pillowcase
and slide them as far under the bed as I can.

I roll out biscuits on the table,
then fix the coffee.
From the garden,
Mr. Oblinger brings cabbage.
"I thought this might round out the meal."
He's got the kind of patchy beard
that says he's new
to prairie living.

Though small,
the cupboard holds
sacks
and
tins.
Mr. Oblinger's been busy,
providing for his bride.

I lay the table,
waiting.
The biscuits grow cold.
I stand at the door,
wave to Mr. Oblinger near the dugout barn.
"The missus inside?" he asks.
I shake my head.

He wipes his face with a handkerchief.
"Wonder where she's gone off to."
Heading to the creek,
he calls for her.
The empty prairie says nothing.
I pretend to study
cabbage,
beans,
a row of potatoes.

Inside I serve up salt pork,
pour coffee,
and wait.

At last
the two walk in.
"Daydreaming out back."

Mr. Oblinger's smile stretches too wide.

Mrs. Oblinger sits,
says nothing.

In bed I think through presidents
and work long division in my head.
It is dark
and quiet,
and the heavy air remains.

I wake to the gray of early dawn
and stay silent as sleep,
so as not to rouse the Oblingers.
But there's no need:
I'm not the only one awake.

The sound is muffled,
like a child at her mother's shoulder.
Just as Hiram can't hold back laughter during
    family prayers,
Mrs. Oblinger's sobs escape the blankets.

Surely Mr. Oblinger hears?
Three of us awake,
two pretending sleep.

Mr. Oblinger stirs,
I duck farther under my sheet,
and, once he's gone,
slip into my work dress.

Relieved to find the water's low,
I grab the bucket.
Outside I breathe in sunshine,
taking care
not to spend
more time than necessary,
but still walking
slowly enough
to study
sky
and
sweep of land,
postponing
the time when I must enter
that closed-in space.

She sits,
her red dress wrinkled,
smoothing tangles from her hair.
I lower the bucket,
straighten,
allowing my shoulders to relax.

"What's that for?" Her eyes accuse me.
"We were out of water," I try.
"Not that," she says.
"Why'd you sigh?"

"I didn't realize—"

"This work too much for you?"
"No, ma'am."
Her eyebrows rise.
"Did you misplace your boots?"
"Mostly I go barefoot,
except for church or snowy days."
"Truly?" she asks.
There is no need to answer.
She can see for herself.

She returns to brushing.

"What happened to your hair?"
I touch my braid,
unraveling.
"My brother cut it on a dare," I say.

She turns away while twisting her curls into a
  bun.
I hear her just the same.
"Stupid girl."

I busy myself at the stove,
put the coffee on,
start in on biscuits,
wonder what Hiram's doing this morning.

Anytime Ma fried up bacon
and turned away from the stove,
Hiram would make a beeline,
grab a piece from the pan,
drop it with a yelp,
suck on his burned fingers.
One morning he pierced a strip with a fork
and waved it to cool,
flinging globs of slippery grease on Ma's
    curtains.
She swatted him with the broom,
shooing him out the door
like an unwelcome badger.

Now Hiram must wait outside until bacon
    frying's done.

Ma's probably rolling dough,
humming.
Maybe Hiram's grinding coffee

now that I'm not there to help.
He's already brought the milk pail in.
When Pa gets back,
he'll share what he heard in town.

I glance up at Mrs. Oblinger,
silent in her rocker,
and turn back to my biscuits,
thankful to be occupied.

Mrs. Oblinger stands when her husband
   enters.
Her hairbrush slips to the ground.
He bends to pick it up
and hands it to her.
"Sorry for the dust.
Once the puncheon floor's in . . ."
He signals toward the door.
"Chapman's got extra wood at his place.
We'll work on it next week."
She lifts her face.
What light there is
brightens her eyes.
"Thank you," she says.

The coffee is bitter,
the biscuits are hard,
the bath water's cold.
Mrs. Oblinger complains but doesn't help.
How did she manage before now?

It's curious.
How am I to know
what to do
when no one is about
much of the time?
Am I to track down the missus
or force Mr. Oblinger
to stop his work?
Or do I act like I am
the one
ordering this household?

Like a shadow,
Mrs. Oblinger floats about,
sometimes outside,
sometimes in.
Is she at the creek fetching water?

This is not my home.
I am the stranger
here.

Beans cook on the stove,
the beds are neat,
the table laid.
I am alone,
my reader before me.

On days I finished chores early,
Ma would let me work lessons before supper.
I'd curl up in the rocker,
my feet tucked under me,
ignoring Ma's scolding
to sit like a lady.
Hiram would perch at the end of his bed,
his elbows on his knees,
my reader in his hands:

"The Grandeur of the Sea"

*What is there more sublime than the trackless,
restless, unfathomable sea? What is there
grander than the calm, gently-heaving,
silent sea?*

With my eyes shut tight,
I'd see the swirling waters,

feel the sea's smooth coolness.
Hiram went over lessons
until I knew them through.
Only then
would I slip into the barn
and try to read what I'd heard to Bessie
until Ma called me for supper.

Mrs. Oblinger comes through the door,
focusing on me,
not one glance at the work I've done.
She opens her mouth as if to speak.
Without a word I close my book;
she turns and walks away.

I think on what Mrs. Oblinger said when I
    first came.
How did she hear about my trouble with
    reading?
Did Pa tell the Oblingers my schooling's
    done,
or did she think a girl my age
who's not in school
mustn't be able to learn?

"The girl's not fit for learning,"
Teacher whispered,
but not quietly enough.
I overheard her
telling the superintendent
during his visit,

"She'll know answers,
but she don't read right."

Not fit,
what Mrs. Oblinger
thinks of me too.

"I'll be leaving early,"
Mr. Oblinger tells us at supper.
"I've got plenty to do in town.
Anything you need?"

"Bring letters!" Mrs. Oblinger pleads.
He touches her cheek.
"I'll see what's at the post office."

After supper Mr. Oblinger pulls me aside.
"You might have noticed
my wife's missing home.
Keep her company tomorrow while I'm away."

I'd rather muck out a barn
barefoot.

"Yes, sir."

It's wet when Mr. Oblinger leaves.
Already there are patches
where the muslin ceiling drips.
I have cleared the breakfast table
and washed up.
There is nothing more to keep me busy.

Mrs. Oblinger sits in her rocker,
lights a candle to bring sense to the dark.
I wonder if the same summer storm
keeps Hiram and Pa inside.

I sit down at the table,
start to mend a shirt.

"I was wrong in trying this,"
Mrs. Oblinger says,
"but his letter was so kind.
I didn't think through prairie living."

She rocks.
"If my brother hadn't shown him my
    photograph,
I wouldn't be stuck here."
I fiddle with a button and thread.

She stops the chair.
Her voice is louder:
"I'm not one of those mail-order brides,
if that's what you're thinking."

I lift my eyes from my sewing.
"No, ma'am," I say.

She rocks again.
"The quiet out here's the worst part,
thunderous as a storm the way
it hounds you
inside
outside
nighttime
day."

I shift to miss a leaking patch forming
    overhead,
hoping she doesn't expect me to talk.
Because what can I say?
The prairie's hard on some,
but it's home to me,
and Mr. Oblinger has tried.

"I hate this place," she whispers.

Before I think better, I say,
"He's left a shade tree out front,
he's plastered the walls,
and he's putting in a proper floor."

"What'd you say?"

Does she even remember I'm here?

"Mr. Oblinger's a good man," I try again.
"He wants to make this home for you."

She stands over me now.
"You think plaster makes a difference in this
    place?
Look at this."
She holds out her mud-caked skirt.
"It's filthy in here!
The ceiling leaks.
Sometimes snakes get through!"

The cool sod's where they like to nest.
"They help with mice," I offer.

She glares.

I want to know how old she is.
(Four years,
maybe five
ahead of me?)
I want her to know
she'll learn to make a home.

"When it's wet outside
and our roof leaks,
Ma and I crawl under the table
and wait for the storm to pass."

She glares again,
but slowly lowers herself to the dry earth.
I settle next to her.

Under the table
we sit,
arms wrapped around our knees,
while water puddles on the bench.
It's possible for a soddy roof to collapse.
I stick my head out.
More soil has gathered in fabric folds,
but the ceiling looks like it will hold.

"Getting hungry?" I ask.
Mrs. Oblinger nods.
I fetch a pot with last night's beans
and hand her a spoon.
We eat in silence,
listening for the wagon and a change
    in the rain.

The even rhythm of the rain lessens.
I pull open the door and step outside.
It's good to feel the open space.

At the creek
the water rushes
where before it was calm.

The missus won't talk to me.
I'm the one who fed her,
thought to bring the quilt
to the only dry spot.
She lies under the table
with her boots on.

I take the linens
and hang them on the line.

Ma's got
her quilts drying.
Hiram's out
to milk the cow.
Pa's turning soil,
grateful for the rainfall.

I'm miles away.

Thank goodness Mr. Oblinger
built this house on a slope.
There is no water at the door.
With it open,
a bit of air
might help to dry the muddy floor
before night comes.

❋

I sleep in the rocker,
the driest spot
besides the makeshift bed,
where Mrs. Oblinger rests.

❋

The coffee's on;
still she doesn't stir.
The creek runs smoothly now.
He should be home soon.

I hear the wagon
and head outside.
It's best if Mr. Oblinger sees me first.

He swings down from the seat.
"How'd you fare?"
"The missus is tired," I say,
unsure of how to explain
why she's not yet left her place
under the table.

She's up now,
sitting at the table.
He's given her the coffee,
thick from waiting on the stove.

She holds a letter,
stares at it for a time,
folds it,
stands,
pushes past the doorway
into sun and open prairie.

Was it real,
that talk we had
the rainy day Mr. Oblinger was in town?
She rarely speaks,
and if she does it's to criticize.
Does she think I like it here?
She's not the only one
missing family,
wishing for familiar voices.
She chose this place.

Can't Mr. Oblinger see
the slow pulling away,
the distance
growing
in this tiny space?
When she sits around back,
I imagine she's counting the miles
between here and home.

Mr. Oblinger and Mr. Chapman
split logs,
lay planks.
I bring out the pail and dipper
and offer them a drink.
Mr. Chapman nods his thanks.
His beard's fuller than Mr. Oblinger's,
but his clothes nonetheless look like town.
Seems like all the folks west of home are new.
Even so,
Pa would approve of their labors.
"Many hands make light work," he'd say.

They labor until the furniture is restored to its
    rightful place.
There is only the entryway to complete.

The men shake hands.
"Much obliged," Mr. Oblinger says.
Mr. Chapman shrugs.
"It's what neighbors do.
I'd appreciate if you could check in on my
    place
once or twice.
I'm going east for a visit,
may not be back before the first snow."

A fine breeze stirs,
the sunflowers nod,
the day she chooses to go riding.
Usually she stays close,
like a tethered calf.

"Pack some biscuits, will you, May?
I want to see all that I can.
The prairie's so beautiful today."
She's never spoken that way before.
"Tell my husband I'll be a while.
Don't count on me for dinner."

When Mr. Oblinger hears,
he smiles.
"It's good to see her happy.
Maybe I'll be done with this floor
before she's back."

I stop Mr. Oblinger as he works
to remind him to eat.
My day's quiet;
I mend
and iron.
I work numbers
and look at a passage in my reader,
the one Hiram helped me with,
about the vastness of the ocean,
the limitlessness of the sea.
His voice in my head helps me when
    I stumble.

I've never seen water spread
straight to the horizon;
these endless grasslands
are sea enough for me.
This soddy's like an island
far from any shoreline.
My home is out there
somewhere.
To me,
a world away.

Maybe because the day is different,
it takes me time to notice
the note
left on the bedside crate,
where she always kept her Bible.

Mr. Oblinger,
You've been so kind,
but I can't stay.
I'm taking the train
back to Ohio.
Please understand.
Louise

I whisper the words,
go through the letter several times,
and I understand.

Mrs. Oblinger's gone.

The biscuits.
She planned to make this look like a simple
    ride,
but she prepared ahead of time.

Mr. Oblinger works;
the floor is almost done,
for her.

I hand him the message.
"The missus left this."

He walks outside to read in the light.
I pull farther back in.
This is his business,
not mine.

I busy my hands with sweeping
the almost-finished floor.

"I need to get to town," he says.
"She probably don't remember the way."
He reaches for his hat
and in his haste
almost trips over the scattered wood.

"Don't worry about supper,"
he says.
"I could be gone some time."

He hitches the other horse to the wagon,
lays his rifle across his knees,
and drives,
fast as lightning sparks fire,
quick as flames consume the prairie.

Even at home,
if Pa and Ma drive into town,
I've got Hiram for company.
And there's Bessie in the barn and the
    laying hens.
Here,
there is no cow yet,
no chickens roosting.
I watch the wagon
until I see nothing on the open plain.
For the first time ever,
I am alone.

Fear flashes inside me.
Pa never left Hiram and me without
    protection.
All around me there is nothing
but the prairie and the sky.
"Silly girl," I tell myself.
"There's no reason to worry."
But it takes a time for my heart to slow.

I stretch out on the grass;
sweet sunshine warms my face.
I stay like this all afternoon.
My chores can wait.

I wake
to evening shadow,
confused.
The wagon is still gone.

Inside I pick an apple from the barrel,
light a candle,
work numbers on my slate.

When I sit up,
my slate falls to the floor.
The candle's burned out.
Morning light filters through the papered
    window.
The other bed is empty.

The missus must have made it far
if they stayed in town overnight.

I have to fetch the water,
gather fuel for the stove.
Some string beans might be ready to pick.

They'll need a good meal
when they return.

I weed the garden
and watch toward town.
Nothing moves against the horizon.

For a time I sit on my heels,
the soddy at my back,
the open prairie before me,
waiting.

There is still no sign of the Oblingers
by the time I've reached the last garden row.
I stand and wipe the dirt
from the front of my dress.

Surely
they'll be back
for supper.

The beans have cooked so long
they are like lumpy corn mush.
I sit in the rocker
with the door open wide.

Maybe something has happened to them.

❋

I dread the blackness
growing stronger outside.

In bed
I hear
the sounds
I miss
when
others
sleep nearby.

The breeze
rattles
at the papered window
and pushes
at the door.

Burrowed
in the quilt,
I hug my knees,
try
not
to listen.

I know there's
something
moving
near the stove.

A mouse,
not
a footstep,
I tell myself.
I would have heard
the wagon
and the welcome sound
of voices.

Gooseflesh ripples
up my arms.
I squeeze my knees tighter.
When
will morning
come?

Maybe Mrs. Oblinger
lost her way,
and her husband never found her.
He could be riding from home to home,
asking after her.

Maybe she rode past town.
Maybe the horse broke its leg.
What if Mr. Oblinger is tired of her?
He might have let her take the train,
and now he's in town,
biding his time.

If Pa knew Mr. Oblinger
had up and left,
he'd rush over to get me,
and when he saw the Oblingers,
he'd give them a tongue-lashing,
for sure.

But Pa
doesn't know,
and I
don't know
what has happened.

What will happen.
Whether I should be
mad,
or scared,
or whether I should prepare a meal:
their welcome supper.

On the fourth day,
I stand at the stove
and, with my finger on the calendar,
trace the days of August.

I've known it since last night:
it's been too long to expect them
to return.

Something's happened.

My legs fold under me
as I try
to catch
my breath
between sobs.

Why would Mr. Oblinger
leave me alone?
Why would that woman
run away?
Why must I be stuck
twice
where I don't want to be,
with no way to tell
Pa, Ma, Hiram,
with
no one
to care for me?

I push open the door
and run,
and run,
and run,
and run,
until the soddy's a tiny speck.
And around me,
the grass reaches in every direction.
There is nothing here to mark my place,
nothing to show me where I am.
No trees.
No stones.
No wagon ruts this way.
Just emptiness.
This isn't home,
where I know the land.

I turn back,
running,
until my surroundings are familiar,
the soddy's larger on the horizon.
I must stay close,
so as to not lose my way.

When the sun is low
and my tears have dried,
I stir from my spot in the grass.
I open the door to the Oblingers' home.
The sudden dark,
cool space
is quiet,
empty,
and strange.

Pa doesn't know they won't return.
The nearest neighbor is gone.

I'm here till Christmas.

Part Two

So many times I've wished for just a minute
to linger
before beginning chores,
or wished I could skip
the washing up after supper—
Now I can do what I want.

No one's going to tell me
to gather fuel
or start the biscuits.
There's no need to cook.
I've got a barrel of apples,
a bit of corn bread left
from yesterday.
I can light the lamp.
No one can tell me I'm being wasteful,
using the light just for schoolwork,
or that it's time for bed.

I can do what I want.

My reader and slate
don't need to be hidden away.
I can keep them out with me.

With an apple in hand,
I open my reader:

I have been infromed—

*I have been informed that stranger the name
Goodman . . .*

The letters aren't working.

*. . . have been informed that a stranger name
Goodman . . .*

I can't place the words where they belong.

*. . . the name of Goodman has settled near you
hope you find in agreeable . . .*

I squeeze my eyes shut,
try to focus.

. . . hope you find him in agreeable . . .

Do it again, May.

. . . find him an . . . find in him an-a
greeble . . .

My fingernails dig into the cover

. . . ana greeable . . .

I fling my reader;
it smacks the wall.

Why can't I do this?
What is
wrong
with me?
I can speak,
and hear,
and see,
and understand when someone reads to me.

I follow lessons at school,
and Ma's directions in the kitchen.
I know what words mean.

So why can't I do this?

I
must
be
stupid.

It is morning.
There is no water,
no fuel.
It was foolish to waste time last night.

A sack of buffalo chips
next to the stove,
water from the stream,
coffee in the pot;
I cannot
let
myself
think.
Just do chores, May.
Keep moving,
go pick some corn.
Maybe I could try to finish the floor
Mr. Oblinger left undone.
There are only a few boards missing.

I bang at the boards,
not sure exactly
where to place each piece,
but figuring with so few to go,
the planks will show me where they belong.

Maybe Mr. Oblinger will
want to fix these boards
to his liking
someday.
I stop myself.

He's never coming back.

I am afraid
in the dark
all alone
I am afraid

It started small:
Hiram's church-going shirt left untucked,
My dirty hands at suppertime.
Then we got bold:
Sneaked a piece of cooling pie,
waded deeper in the stream
than Pa allowed.

Somehow Hiram rarely caught trouble.
That smile of his softened Ma.
Pa, grateful for extra hands,
overlooked the times Hiram forgot to milk,
misplaced the saw,
dropped his boot in the creek.

I thought of something he wouldn't dare do.
"Get Ma's scissors
and meet me out back."

It was just the two of us behind the soddy,
but I leaned in close.
"Cut some of my hair."

He narrowed his eyes.
"Why'd I want to do that?"

"Afraid Ma will notice?" I sang.
"Worried Pa will tell you
to wait for him in the barn?"

"You're daring me?" he asked.

"I am," I said.

That was enough to stir him.
And when he grabbed at a braid
and the scissors snapped,
I scooped it up,
a four-inch rope of brown hair.
Swishing it under his nose, I told him,
"You're going to get it tonight."

That smile of his lit up his face.
"Don't I know it."

I swatted at him with the braid,
yelled, "I'm showing Ma!"
and ran.

It is not strange
to wear the same dress
from day to day,
but to awake,
still clothed,
and not notice
until the coffee's made—

I hope Mrs. Oblinger fell off that horse
and is still wandering the prairie.
Mr. Oblinger
better be dead.

Pa deserves the mess he's made,
sending me here.
His only daughter
abandoned
by strangers,
forgotten
by family,
left behind
by classmates,
ignored
by Teacher.

Nobody cares
about me.

I hate this place.

Today,
if it takes forever,
I will see the place
where the earth touches sky.
I will find it.
I will track it down.
I will not sit here and wait
for nobody to come,
for nothing to happen.
Have Hiram and I been wasting time
on a foolish game?
Today,
I will learn the truth.

❋

Over my shoulder I check for the soddy
one time,
two times,
three.
Why did I think I'd be brave enough
to set out on my own?

How did Hiram and I
get this idea anyway?

The earth is round,
Miss Sanders told us.
She brought that globe to school,
let us pass it around.

If stories were true,
I'd follow a bread-crumb path
all the way home.

But I have no heart for fairy tales
anymore.

I return to the soddy,
gather pebbles at the creek,
and line them up,
a family of smooth stones.
One by one
I heave them into the water,
harder,
then harder still,
until I'm wet,
and hoarse from yelling,
and done with childish dreams.

I have decided
there is no need to iron
my dresses
or the linens.
And my hair,
I don't have to pull it back
in a braid.
My coffee
doesn't need to be hot.

Who will notice?

I think it might be September,
if I've counted right.

64

Some days I sit at the creek,
the sun on my back,
collecting pill bugs
from under rocks.
They curl into a ball at the slightest touch,
then,
waiting,
unfold themselves to continue their journey,
this time on my wrist,
my thumb,
the frayed cuff of my dress.

I hold them,
watch them rush,
wonder
what sort of task could hurry
such a creature along.

I lie in the sunshine,
thankful
for the freshness of the grass,
the babbling company of the stream.

Some days I sit in the rocker,
the quilt about me though it's hot outside.
I shun the sunlight,
groan to think of the water I must fetch,
the steps I'll have to take,
the work that's needed
just to exist.

Wouldn't it be better
to
forget
to
care?

Wouldn't it be easier
to stay in the hazy place where dreams come,
to simply fade away?

I crouch under the table,
listening
to the rain
drip on the supper dishes I left out
in my rush
to stay dry.

My thoughts drift back to Teacher.
I can't let them happen
here,
under the table,
where there's no task to keep me busy.

The bedding is wet.
I try to find a way to sleep
that allows for comfort,
but I can't.
My memories catch up with me.
I wonder what Teacher had to say
when I didn't return to school?

*"The girl's finally got some sense,
staying home."*

Maybe I was only smart before Teacher came.

It's because you won't try.

Teacher,
I've tried more than you will ever know,
out in the barn,
with my book,
and my voice
shaking.

The words on paper
don't match the sounds I make.
I have to memorize
to even try to read aloud.

So
if you think I can't read,
Teacher,
then maybe you're right.

Coffee,
a half sack of dried beans,
flour, sugar, and cornmeal.
The sugar's not good for much
when eating simple things.
But the flour—
with my bit of sourdough starter—
keeps providing for biscuits
like I used to bake
with Ma.

The last of the meat ran out long ago.

A tin of peaches
is all that is left
of Mrs. Oblinger's fine things.
I've told myself I must hold out longer
before I touch them.
They're stashed,
like a promise,
behind the rest.

I pull the door open,
stand with my hands on my hips,
and yell into the morning:
"Guess what, Mrs. Oblinger?
I don't think you're too bright
yourself!"

What does it matter if she can't hear me?
If it was long ago
she called me stupid?

"Hope you enjoyed your ride
on that lovely prairie day!"

I lift my dusty skirts,
sashay like someone fancy,
curtsy to the cabbage,
think on the missus and her eastern ways:
good riddance.

I have almost eaten
to the bottom of the apple barrel.

When the world is black,
I'm most alone,
the silence thick around me.
I pray for wind,
for rain,
for the meadowlark
to break
the constant pound of quiet.

What is that?
What is at the door?

A rasping sound,
a muffled breath,
a whine
outside.
Then, nothing.

My pulse surges through my fingertips
as I crack open the door.
Scratches line the heavy wood,
yellow threads cut deeply in the boards.

There are tracks
on the edge of the moonlit garden.

A wolf has been here.
I am not alone.

Avery Pritchard told me
that when his pa's away
at night,
sometimes a pack of wolves surrounds their
   soddy.
The wolves sense a difference about the place.
They howl,
they scratch,
but mostly,
they sit and wait.
Can they smell that someone's missing?
Do they sense the fear inside?

Mrs. Pritchard tells the children stories,
presses her forehead against the windowpane,
and says, "Get on, you!"

Last spring,
in the early dawn,
Mrs. Pritchard took the shotgun
and waited by the door.
When she heard the wolf pack stirring,
she aimed and fired.
The pack rolled off like summer storm clouds.
One skinny female lay dead.

Avery's ma dragged that wolf to the door
and left it,
a hairy mound,
at the entrance to their soddy.
All day she stepped over it
when she went to milk
or fetch water.
She wouldn't let anyone else outside.

When Mr. Pritchard arrived,
she didn't say a word,
just handed him the shovel
and shut the door.

Avery's pa buried the wolf out back.

Now,
when he has business in town,
he makes sure to hurry home
come nightfall.

Mr. Oblinger
took the rifle.

When Miss Sanders came
to teach our school,
she was the first to understand
I could get the words
from the book
to my mind
more easily if I listened to lessons.

She didn't force me to read
in front of everyone.

Once she brought me
a book about a boy named Tom Sawyer
because she thought I'd find Tom like Hiram.
She read it during recess
just for me.

But when Miss Sanders married,
she left our school
and Teacher came.

The garden has given up
its last yield.
Some withered string beans,
a dozen potatoes,
five ears of corn,
one small head of cabbage,
crawling with bugs.

Days and nights run together.
Sometimes I forget how
I got to this place
or why I am still here.

Maybe it is October?

There was frost
this morning,
but it melted quickly.

❉

There's no time left for waiting.
There is nothing holding me here.
I can't abide this place any longer.

80

I pack my pillowcase:
one extra dress wrapped around my worthless
    reader,
one stocking filled with corn bread,
one with biscuits.
On top of this,
two ears of corn
and a cup.

I button Ma's fine boots.
I wish I had insisted on keeping Hiram's old
    ones,
but I know Ma gave me hers
for herself as much as me,
a message to Mrs. Oblinger,
fresh from the city,
showing that women out here still have some
    grace.
My feet will hurt, I reckon,
before I make it far.

The broom's my only weapon.
I think on Ma,
the way she swatted Hiram when he snatched
    the bacon.

❧ 110 ❧

I grasp the handle,
throw my pillowcase over one shoulder,
and step out onto the prairie.

How did Pa get here?
I see nothing to point the way.
I walk alongside the Oblingers' little creek,
hoping it will lead to the river,
to a neighbor,
to the outskirts of town.

The grass has dried to silver-green;
it slaps my legs as I push forward.
Sweat trickles between my shoulder blades.
Impossible to think there was frost just
    this morning.

I have only the stream
and endless grasses to guide me.

Sometimes I see wagon ruts,
a memory pressed in dried mud.
If western Kansas had more folks,
this would be easier.
There might be a well-worn path by now.

Grasshoppers whir,
fly about me.
I swat at them with the broom.

My stomach clenches,
so I shake some crumbled corn bread from
    the stocking
straight into my mouth.
Then up ahead,
I spot the jagged branches of a currant bush.
Late-summer birds have picked over
the berries that remain.
I grab at what's left,
red-black juice staining my fingers,
eating,
eating,
pocketing the dry ones,
squatting until my knees ache.

I stand and stretch,
look behind me,
recognizing nothing.
Something rustles,
and I reach for the broom.
Like me,
the animal freezes.
We stay that way
until my shoulders throb.

Then
a jackrabbit leaps beside me.
I drop the broom,
fall back,
glimpse it dashing zigzag.

My breath comes short
and painful.
"It was a rabbit," I say,
but the words mean nothing
to the weakness creeping up my legs.

Here's what's true:
Already
the evening sky is pushing back the daylight.

Gooseflesh tingles on my arms.
I don't know where I am,
I can't know where I'm going.

And suddenly,
I'm running
back!
I'm running—
my heels slam into the hard-packed earth.
Running—
my breath's jagged.
Running—
birds scatter from their grass nests.
I need those walls around me!
The pillowcase slaps my back.

Pain rips through my ankle.
I tumble to the ground
and curse the hole I've stepped in.

The sky is almost black when,
limping,
I reach the soddy.

My ankle's purple.
Those stupid boots.

Fetching water today,
I catch a glimpse of myself in the stream:
hair hanging in clumps,
dress ripped at one shoulder.
I haven't used the washtub since
the Oblingers left.
My eyes study the dirty girl.

I finger the last few currants
still in my pocket.
Maybe I could go back and check for more.
If I hadn't been startled,
if I'd stuck it out a little longer,
I'd have bulging apron pockets.
Maybe I'd have reached another soddy.
That neighbor Mr. Chapman's gone,
but if I'd found his place,
surely he'd have some jerky,
a tin of soda crackers left behind.

But now,
with this ankle,
I can't go far.
And the wolf.
I shiver,
remembering how frightened I was
of just a little rabbit.

I sit beside the stream
dipping my fingers in the icy water.
In summer,
Pa and Hiram bring in trout,
speckled bodies writhing

in their hands.
I trail my fingers,
wiggling them like Hiram showed me.
Nothing happens.

I run,
holding my skirts above my knees.
I holler
and skip
and make faces at the outhouse.
I slam the door,
take a spoon to the pots and pans.

I whistle,
I spit,
think up as many unladylike things as I can,
and do them.

Out in the open.
For the whole empty world to see.

A thin sheet of ice crept across
the water pail last night.
I take the dipper and push through
to scoop a drink,
then stir the fire
for breakfast.

❋

The sky
holds the high white
of snow.
It is too early
for this.
I am not ready.

Maybe there won't be a storm
after all.
Autumn is devious.
Calm afternoons with no hint of breaking
can turn violent,
bringing wind,
ushering in rain
and even snow.

Or maybe I haven't been paying enough
    attention
and I'll get trapped out here
in
a
blizzard.

On
my
own.

Maybe May B.
Maybe

Snow is falling.
Why did I not prepare
when the weather first turned?
I have left
so many things
undone.
Maybe I should check the garden
for one last potato.
I should have gathered more chips to burn
yesterday.

Wind runs across the prairie,
swirling snowflakes and brittle grass.
I push through the icy gale,
force open the barn door.

Only one bale of hay is still intact.
I squat to lift it,
hardly seeing where I'm going,
and make it to the soddy more by memory
than sight.
My sore ankle complains.

Back in the barn,
I kneel in the scattered hay,
scooping armfuls into my dress,
and press the hem against my waist.
Outside again,
the blinding white whips at my eyes.
I bend my head for some protection.
Snow gathers at the soddy door.
I shove it open with a shoulder,
dump the hay,
and turn toward the barn
again and again,
until what hasn't blown away

is scattered
across the puncheon floor.

Once,
after weeks of rain,
Pa had Hiram and me
twist hay
into bundles for burning.

Now I sit in almost-darkness,
binding hay in logs
that won't flame out,
as just a handful would.

Stepping over
piles of hay bundles,
bits of loose grass,
I reach into the barrel

for the last apple.

For a moment I think
I've left the lamp burning,
but the brightness isn't
exactly the same.
Around me,
it's as clear as midday,
The papered window alight.

I slip out of bed.
Bits of hay stick to my feet
as I pull open the door.
A thin layer of snow blankets the entrance,
sparkling in the morning sun.

❋

If only
I'd not panicked that day
I tried to go.
But with the snow,
it's too late to consider again.

Whether or not I want to be here,
I am.

The sun is out.
Ma's boots leave
soft gray marks
in the melting snow.
It is too early for
winter to last.

I will be ready next time.

93

My arm pricks as I lower it into the stream;
the water's even colder than before.
I press my body to the bank,
trying to cast no shadow,
reaching deeper with my hand.

Why did I never try for fish with Pa
    and Hiram?

Soon I can hardly feel
my wiggling fingers,
but I keep moving,
hoping trout will notice.

Something flits below the surface,
curves gracefully,
slips by.
I watch for movement farther upstream
and let my fingers dance
like moss,
like water bugs,
like tadpoles beating tiny tails.

Then I spy one!
It's smooth,

a ribbon of color
running
down its middle.

My fingers wave;
it approaches.
I am close enough to stroke its belly,
and with one quick jerk,
I grab that fish and throw it on the bank.

Three fish—
My stomach's full
for the first time in weeks.

I've thought through arithmetic
and worked some problems on my slate.
I've recited states
alphabetically
and
in the order of their joining the Union.

My reading I've avoided
ever since that day
nothing worked right.

Lamplight shines on my book,
its blue cover frayed at the corners,
the spine a lighter shade
in the middle
where my hand grips,
finger smudges on the back.

I examine it like it's the first time
Ma handed it to me,
the reader she brought
all the way to Kansas.

She didn't know then,
I didn't know,

the tricks words would play
on me.

What if I were to pretend
the struggles never happened?
What if I were to open this book,
go back,
start
fresh?

My fingers feel almost as chilled as they did
this afternoon
under the water,
but didn't I pull three fish to the surface?
Didn't I gut them,
cook them up,
and eat my fill?

Surely
these words
can't be as difficult
to grasp,
as slippery to work with.

I find the page that tripped me weeks ago,

press along the spine.

I shut my eyes,
breathe deeply,
tell myself nothing will change
or surprise me
when I open my eyes.

No one is listening.

I have need—

No.

I have been in formed that a stragner . . .
a stranger
named Goodman . . .

Slowly, May,
don't go on what you remember.
The words begin to swim,
but I hold fast.
Just one sentence to push through.

. . . have been informed that a stranger

of the name of Goodman has settled near you.

I press the cover closed with both hands.
My heart thrums
as I turn down the lamp,
slip into bed,
filled to bursting.

From the calendar I tear away
one month,
then two.
Is it October
or November?

Time was made
for others,
not for someone
all alone.

The fish rest deeper now.
I cook beans day after day.
Sometimes I bake corn bread,
but the meal's getting low.

If I eat just a little,
there will be food for weeks to come.
My mind knows this,
but my fingers shake with every bite,
and I've taken to checking my rations
over and over,
licking my finger,
sweeping it under the cornmeal sack,
hoping for a few more grains.

The tin of peaches,
still tucked behind the sugar,
I won't open until I must.

I pull it down from the shelf,
hold it in my hand.
"Peaches," I read aloud.
"Fresh picked."
My voice sounds funny,
like that odd instrument

Mr. Wolcott brought to the literary social
   last year.
He pulled and squeezed
the black thing;
it opened like a folded piece of cloth.
Accordion,
I think he called it.
"Peaches.
Fresh picked," I say again.

I move my finger under each word:
"Peaches.
Fresh picked!"

Ma would be horrified,
but Ma's not here to see
I've slept most of the morning away.
It would be nice
to lounge and doze
as long as I feel like staying abed,
but it's more burden than comfort
because of all the time to remember:

When Teacher came,
I hoped she would be
like Miss Sanders,
but I should have known
from the start:
Teacher
wasn't the same.

"I want to see what each of
you is capable of," Teacher announced,
even before she sat down.
"Youngest ones first.
We'll work our way to the top of the school."
With a ruler she pointed to the first row.
"Stand and recite the alphabet."

Jemmy Thompson's lip
turned down,
the way a newborn's
does before it starts wailing,
but he managed to make it through.

"Older grades."
Teacher eyed us in the back.
Rita Howard had to start over three times,
her voice too soft
for Teacher's liking.
Teacher scolded Hiram for rushing
through his piece.

And then it was my turn.
I opened to "The Voice of the Wind."
With Hiram's help,
I'd read it through just the night before.

Did Teacher sense
what everyone thought
as I walked—
knees like water—
to the front of the room?
Their thoughts weren't audible,

but I heard them just the same.

I took a deep breath.
Maybe this time I could do it.
Maybe Teacher would never have to know.

I held my reader in front of me,
high enough so I wouldn't have to see
    their faces,
both elbows squeezed to my sides.

   "I am the when.
   Wind.
   I am wind and I . . ."

Rita covered her mouth
with her prissy little fingers.

   ". . . I am the wind and I—"

Teacher rapped the ruler on her desk.
"Excuse me, child.
What is your name?"

Warm tears splashed my feet.

Something was broken inside.
My new teacher knew.

Just like my reading,
my words were slow to form.
"May-vis, ma'am."

"Well, May-vis," she said,
like my name tasted sour,
"I think you're sitting in the wrong part
of the schoolroom.
Kindly move to the second row."

"Ma'am?"
I turned my head just a little,
not wanting to show my tears.
She was seating me with the little ones?

"I said"—
she spoke louder now,
like I was hard of hearing—
"move to the front of the room."

I glanced at Hiram.
He shrugged,

but his eyes hardly met mine.
I fetched my slate
and slid in next to Jemmy,
whose feet didn't yet meet the floor.

It's the noise that wakes me
in the darkness close as a shroud.
Wind whips about the soddy;
I imagine I hear the walls groan.

Prairie quiet
is rarely silent.

Mrs. Oblinger called it
lonely wailing;
it made her fret and talk of home.

I feel my way across the room.
Just cracking the door open
drives fresh snow over my feet.

For all Mrs. Oblinger's fussing,
she'd never seen what the worst prairie
    winds bring,
what is coming—
I wipe at tears I haven't noticed until now.

Blizzard.

Stumbling toward the stove,
I reach for my jar of starter.
It can't freeze;
I'll need biscuits.

In bed I huddle in a ball,
two quilts about me,
the starter jar against my chest.

The first time I heard the chant
was the recess after Teacher moved me
to the front
with the babies
missing their ma,
still losing their milk teeth,
swinging their legs when Teacher
   looked away.

When Teacher dismissed us from lessons,
I met Hiram at the farthest edge of the
   schoolyard.
"I don't think you need to worry none.
She'll figure out you're smart real soon.
May Betts, don't let her get to you."
He had that look that reminds me
someday he'll be a man.

Behind us I thought
I heard my name.

May B.
May B.

I turned around,

but no one was calling.

"Let's go play."
Hiram gave me a shove.

We picked sides pretty quick
until it got to me.
Rita whined to Avery,
"Maybe May will freeze in the middle of
    the game,
just like she did this morning."

"May B. can play just fine,"
Nathaniel said, tossing the ball in the air.
"Keep the picks going."

"Maybe she can, maybe she can't."
Rita stared straight at me.

Some of the little ones started up:
"Maybe she can, maybe she can't. . . ."

Avery said,
"May's good and you know it."
He beckoned to me.

"Come join us."
Rita scowled.

"Maybe she can, maybe she can't,
Maybe she can, maybe she can't. . . ."

I turned away,
the taunt following me to the schoolhouse.

The air is still
when I awake.
I remember immediately:
blizzard.

The door won't budge
with the first tug
or the second.

I press my foot against the wall,
yank one last time.
A barrier of blue-white snow
stands solid.

Slamming the door,
I spin around,
press my back against it.
There is so little space
to live in,
to draw in air,
to move.
The walls hold everything so close.

I need to get out!

Swinging the door open again,
I dig like a prairie dog.

When Hiram and I had snowball fights,
I hated the feel
of snow trapped at my wrists
between mittens and coat.
Now it slips down my sleeves,
gathers in the elbows of my dress,
and I don't pay it any mind.
I have to get out of here.

I dig until my fingers throb.
I dip them in the pail,
and the icy water
burns like liquid fire.
But slowly I am able to move my hands.

Looking over my shoulder,
I see the mound
heaped on the floor
and the useless hole
I've dug.

I clench the pail in my reddened hands

bent like claws
and throw it at the hole.
Water splatters everything—
the table,
yesterday's beans,
even the twisted hay in the basket
and the precious few buffalo chips.
How could I have done something so
    thoughtless?

"Stupid girl."
If Mrs. Oblinger could see me now.

"The girl's not right,"
Teacher would say.
"Something don't work proper in her head."

I grip my reader,
open it to the middle,
rip a handful of paper from the spine.
My numb hands fumble at the stove
    door latch.
I tug it open
and watch the pages burn.

"This is what a Maybe gets!"
I shout.

Sobbing,
I sink to the floor;
the rough wood scrapes my knees
as I crawl back to bed
and bury myself under the quilts.

"I won't," I told Teacher.

She lifted my chin with a finger.
"You won't or you can't?"

I felt my cheeks flame
there in front of everyone,
all those eyes
examining me like an oddity,
some abnormal thing.

"I won't," I said again.

She thrust the book before me,
the copy Miss Sanders had left behind.
"Read it," she said.

Hiram's lips moved,
saying something I couldn't follow.
Everyone waited,
staring at me.
My insides clenched.

It was the chapter where Tom returns,
witnesses his own funeral.

So many complicated words
too easy to trip on.
I kept my mouth closed,
tried to keep my breathing calm.

Teacher's voice got higher. "Well?"

She stood there,
waiting to pounce at my first mistake.
Wanting to make a fool of me,
ready to show how stupid I was.

"I won't!" I shouted at her.

She gripped my wrist
and I was thankful
for the pain,
thankful
for an excuse
to cry.

"Then kindly find your way home.
Only come back when you're ready to learn."

What if I'd read that first paragraph perfectly?

She'd have argued I'd had Hiram whisper
  answers.

She never believed I could,
anyhow.

I am going to stay here,
wrapped in these quilts,
let the fire die,
and freeze to death
or maybe starve,
whichever comes first.
Then Pa will be sorry
for sending me here.
Was it worth
those few dollars
to find
your daughter dead?

I peek out of the quilts
at the snow mound on the floor.
The cold pinches at my nose.
The stove spits out so little warmth,
I choose to stay abed,
freezing,
rather than risk the chill in moving
from bed to fire.

It was a good reading day,
that afternoon I asked Miss Sanders.
We'd worked all recess together,
my voice sure and strong.

She'd always told me she believed in me,
that I could make the reading happen,
to give it time
and practice.
Now she sat at her desk,
preparing for our after-recess lesson.

"Do you think I could earn a teaching
      certificate
once I'm old enough?"

Miss Sanders,
always brimming with kindness,
fiddled at her desk far too long.

"I'm sorry, May, what was that?"
But
her face said,
Please don't ask me again,
don't make me tell you something
that will only bring you hurt.

"It's nothing," I said,
and forced a smile.
"It's time for lessons.
I'll go ring the bell."

So many things
I know about myself
I've learned from others.
Without someone else to listen,
to judge,
to tell me what to do,
and to choose
who I am,
do I get to decide for myself?

Have I slept
or have I been awake all this time?
If Ma were here she'd say,
"May, get moving.
The day's not for resting."

With the quilts around me,
I shuffle across the floor
to the pot of leftover beans.
A layer of ice has formed
over them.
I don't care.
I crack it with a spoon
and hunch,
shivering,
swallowing without tasting at all.

I squeeze a hay log,
to feel if the cold
is ice
or just the air.
Only two logs don't crackle
the way the popcorn
in the skillet does.
The fire has burned so low,

I have to push it along,
stirring and blowing
before I place the hay logs
gently on the embers.
A lick of flame
grows brighter,
and I draw up close enough
to burn my eyebrows.

I am
Mavis Elizabeth Betterly.
I am
used to hard work.
I can
run a household better
than Mrs. Oblinger ever could.
What does it matter,
those things
that
hold me back?

What does it matter
when I make mistakes?
They don't
make me
who
I
am.

I search through Mrs. Oblinger's sewing box.
In front of her tiny looking glass,
I run my fingers through my hair,
then grip a handful
and cut.
The scissors snap
as sheaves fall loose upon the floor.

Samson didn't get to choose
what Delilah did,
tricking him into the haircut that sapped
   his strength.

I didn't ask
to read like a child,
quit school,
come here,
starve.

One last snip,
and the last strands
drop.
My hair is short.
Jagged.
I

made it this way,
not someone else.
I
chose
to hack it off.
This is of my own doing.

I grasp handfuls of hair,
Shove it
into the stove,
watch it
curl,
shrivel,
and burn.

It is time to figure out
how to care for myself,
not by waiting
or trying to forget I've been left here.
Living now,
not later on when Pa comes.
Not last year in my memory.

I bang ice from the hay logs.
The few buffalo chips must stay as they are,
too fragile to pound on the floor.
My hands move like wet leather
dried out in the sun.

I've taken to using my coat as another blanket;
my mittens I wear all the time;
I haven't removed Ma's boots for days.
Mr. Oblinger has clothing
stored beneath their bed,
and there's Mrs. Oblinger's trunk.
I'm not ready to root through
their underdrawers.
I will make do with what I have.

I study the soddy.

I've neglected to wash Mrs. Oblinger's pots.
Footprints cover the floor.
The bed's disheveled.

I straighten the cupboards
and find that can of peaches.

I place the tinned peaches on the table,
shake out the quilts,
folding them over the back of the rocker,
and sweep up the mess of dirt
on the floor.
With the broom I push snow into
    Mrs. Oblinger's pots,
to use later for washing.
The pail I fill also
and place near the stove.

I continue sweeping,
but can't push from my mind
stories I've heard:
people caught off guard in a blizzard
who wander,
looking for shelter,
lost for days
just yards from home.
The freezing starts in hands and feet,
then comes a sleep
with no waking.

I don't know what it is that reminds me
of the sourdough starter
still in the jar on the bed.
Surely it's frozen.
If I'd left it at the back of the stove,
the dough would still be
warm enough to work with.
I scoop up the jar.
The cold bites through my mittens,
but I must warm it myself.
The stove top would be too sudden.

I drag the rocker to the fire and sit,
climb into the quilts again,
and place the starter jar in my pillowcase,
doubling up the fabric.

Ma must be singing
"Old Dan Tucker" or "Home, Sweet Home"
right about now
as she boils potatoes.
Hiram's tooling leather,
maybe joining in the song:

No more from that cottage again will I roam,

Be it ever so humble, there's no place like home.

Pa's found a way out to the barn,
or if not,
he's working toward a way.

I imagine Ma and her broom
behind me
keeping time with the rocker.

I roll the starter jar
in my lap
the same way I scrub at laundry
on the washboard.
Back and forth,
my back hunched,
a tight pinch in my shoulders.

Sometimes Miss Sanders asked me to read
just to her.
The words would come more easily
without a full room watching.
Other times it would be just as difficult
as any other day.
She never lost patience
or said,
"We've been over this story again and again;
why can't you read it now?"
She'd say,
"Maybe tomorrow
the words will come right."
Or,
"Slower, May,
no need to rush. Take your time.
Let the words form

before you speak them."

Sometimes we would read together,
and those times my words were almost right,
her voice leading,
though still in step with mine.
I felt the rhythm of the words.
I heard the sounds needed to make them.
They didn't stick together or jumble on
    the page.

The starter is softer now.
I add it to the flour and roll out biscuits.

The calendar is tattered,
its corners curled and browned
from dirty hands
and moist prairie air.
I check to see where time might be,
though I stopped marking days
long ago.
For every month I'm sure I've spent at the
    Oblingers',
I subtract a week,
so as not to raise my hopes too high.

If Pa knew,
he'd be here,
faster than any train,
any buffalo stampede from the early
    prairie days,
faster than Hiram at school races,
to take me home.

I remove the pots from the stove,
letting the water cool just a bit,
then scrub at the crusted film left behind.
Mess slops on the floor;
wet patches bloom on the bodice of my dress.
I have no place to throw this filth,
no water to rinse clean.
For the first time since the blizzard morning,
I pull open the door,
dreading to see things left as they were before.

A shiny layer of ice on the solid wall of snow
reminds me of the water I threw.

With the broom handle,
I stab and pick
until I've made
a deeper hole.
I pour in the wash water.
The space stretches just a little.

I fill the pots with the snow I've scattered
and put them on the stove.

The snow muffles all noise,
so I am surprised when I hear the sound
   outside.
Scratching,
not the same as before,
that was dry claws
on dry boards.
Softer now,
like a rake dragged over freshly cut hay,
this scratching is persistent,
more urgent.

The wolf.

Can he smell the little food I have left?
But I know better.
He has no interest in corn bread and beans.
Wolves are carnivores.
They hunt rabbits, buffalo.
Pa's careful of an evening to bring Bessie to
   the barn.

Pain claws at my middle.
I know hunger too.

I'm as hollow as a washtub
turned over to dry.
I could make some biscuits,
or lick a handful of sugar,
but I reach for the peaches,
the last special treat
left by the Oblingers.

I trace my fingers over
Fresh picked
and say the words at the same time.

Sometimes with Miss Sanders,
I'd try different ways to read.
Once I held the rag she used
to wipe the blackboard.
When I struggled with a sound,
I'd squeeze the grimy cloth into a ball
and try again.
I don't know how,
but it helped the letters fall into place.

When Teacher came I'd focus so hard,
trying to imagine that balled-up rag.
I was ashamed

to stand with the little ones
in the front of the room.
I knew more than any of them,
more than Rita,
and Avery,
and Hiram,
put together.

Those days
I'd stumble some,
other times I'd make it through,
my fingernails leaving half-moons in my palm.

The peaches are cold,
smooth,
sweet.
I eat them with an ache in my stomach,
and swallow like Ma herself
spooned them up.

The buffalo chips are gone;
these hay twists must last.
No amount of modesty can keep me
from going through Mrs. Oblinger's trunk.

I pull at a corner of bright fabric
until it spreads across my lap.
The red dress.
Did Mrs. Oblinger make it back to Ohio?
I pull her dress over the three I already wear
and smooth it down,
remembering her soft hands,
oval fingernails,
never broken on a scrub board.
She hated me,
I think.
She thought I hated her.
Did I,
really?
Were we so very different?

I take a pair of Mr. Oblinger's stockings
and wear them over my mittens.

I wrap his muffler around my head,
burrow in the quilts and coat,
and rock before the stove.

Last night I dreamed Pa'd come
to get me.
He'd brought a shovel and dug,
scraping the snow
like a farmer breaking ground.

Again I rinse the pots.
The dishwater stretches
the opening in the snow wall
each time I pour it in.
The pots grow heavier
as I lift them.
What I wouldn't give for a bite of meat,
or that bug-infested cabbage.

I hope for a hint of light
reaching through the hole,
a reminder of the world outside.

Since the blizzard day,
I haven't opened my reader,
but now,
with a small scoop of beans
on the stove
and two biscuits from yesterday,
I sit in the rocker before the fire,
thankful for hot coffee,
and for the flicker of light
cast on the cover
of my book.

The pages fall open in my lap,
the spine empty in the center
where I ripped the paper out.
I flip back to see
which poems remain:
"Home and Its Memories,"
"The Battle of Hastings,"
"Light Out of Darkness."
I glance up at this last title,
taking in the shadows around me.
In this place,
I've met darkness like never before.
I understand light

because of these months
here.

I know this book,
remember what comes after each piece,
so that as I'm turning through,
I feel the space of missing pages getting
    nearer.
I know what shares the other side of "Light
    Out of Darkness."

Most of "The Voice of the Wind" is intact.
I run my finger under each word,
The ones that cost me my place at school,
that filled me with despair.

I know it by heart,
but I read it anyway,
trust my voice to lead me word by word:

  I am
  the wind,
  and I
  blow,
  blow,

blow,
Driving
the rain
and the
beautiful
snow;

I go slowly,
invite the words to find
a home
between
each breath.

No one is here
to listen,
or laugh.
I'm not whispering,
not mumbling,
I own this poem.

> *Making confusion*
> *wherever I go;*
> *Roaring*
> *and moaning,*
> *Wailing and groaning.*

The words come faster.
Sometimes I twist them,
have to stop and try again.
But why should there be shame in that?
I'm doing it!
I'm reading!

> *Rounding the hill-top, I rush down the dale,*
> *Ruffling the river that waters the vale,*
> *Driving before me the white-winged sail.*

The first three stanzas remain,
the fourth left halfway:

> *'Cross desolate deserts I wildly roam;*
> *Wand'ring earth's corners, where nothing calls*
> *home,*
> *I whisper in secret; I watch all alone,*

I know the rest I threw in the fire,
how the wind can lull,
can cheat and trick.
But today,
it's my turn to make my own ending.

Part Three

I tuck a finger inside my reader
and reach for the basket of hay twists.

There are three left.

I need a plan.

I hold my bundled hands
against the stove door,
taking every last bit of heat
before I leave the rocker.

My feet are small enough
to wear three sets of stockings,
even if one boot doesn't button properly
over the ankle I twisted months ago.

I pocket the last two biscuits.
They will need to last me.

Pa's coming,
but I don't know when.

I shove the broom handle up
into the icy hole beyond the door
again
and again
until my shoulders burn.

Nothing changes.
Maybe if I took a spoon,
put it in the stove,
wrapped the handle in a bit of cloth,
I could
slowly
dig
my
way
out.

That wolf is somewhere out there.

I burn myself through cloth and stockings.
The spoon's heat is drawn almost instantly
once it touches snow.

What melts drips down my sleeves.
I return to the stove,
heat the spoon,
scrape,
scrape,
scrape,
until I've formed a hole deep enough
to try the broom handle again.
And though I thrust the handle with all
    I have left,
the snow ceiling still doesn't budge.

Maybe it is senseless digging out.
I am fifteen miles from home,
a distance a body could cover in one day
if nourished
and warm
and familiar with the way.
I might as well set out for the Pacific;
it's so big,
I reckon it would be easier to find.

My cropped hair falls across my face.
Senseless or not,
I will do what I have to,
what is right,
this moment,
for me.

How long do I heat the spoon,
pick at the snow,
swing the broom handle?
I'm shouting
like the wall will listen,
"Stupid blizzard. Danged ice!"
My hands blister beneath their layers.

The hole is big as my head.

How deep is this snow?

I've been so careful
not to waste the candles,
but that time is over now.

There are two left,
almost stubs.
I light one,
hold it in the snow hole.
Water drips
and the candle sputters out.
I light the second one and set it on the table,
then touch them wick to wick.
Every time the flame goes out,
I light my candle
and hold it to the snow again.

It is hard to tell what is sun,
what is candle,
what is pure hope.

The sound of the broomstick
against the snow
is less like a drum.
This is the soft thump
of kneading bread.

I swing the handle
faster and harder
with a power that has waited until now.

Suddenly
the broom handle sticks,
and I must yank it loose.
Snow tumbles down,
blessing me like
a downpour on parched fields.

The sky is blue!

I slip into my coat,
pack my pillowcase,
then straighten the soddy before I go.
If Mr. Oblinger does return someday,
I want him to find things in their proper
    places:
the bench tucked under the table,
the rocker angled properly.
There is nothing I can do with the dirty
    bean pot
except fill it with fresh snow.
I leave one quilt folded
over the back of the rocker.
The other will offer some protection outside.

I cling to the lower lip of the hole with one
    hand
and dig the toe of my boot into the snow wall,
heaving the quilt,
then the pillowcase
up and out,
and last of all,
the broom.

The sun is low in the east,
the sky is clear;
I begin.

I walk toward the morning sun,
glancing over my shoulder at the mound
   of snow
that is the soddy.
Soon,
it is impossible to say what is house
and what is prairie.

There's no creek to guide me.
Nothing is familiar,
but I push forward still.

Ma's dainty boots don't make walking easy,
but I am grateful for their cover.
Ice slips into the place I left unbuttoned,
and I tug one sock
and try to fasten a few buttons more.

There.
Just to my right,
paw prints in the snow.

He's still out here.
Was he separated from his pack?
Is he the weak one?
Has he eaten since the storm?

I secure the pillowcase
within the bodice of the red dress.
The quilt's folded over my coat,
wrapped from shoulders to elbows,
my threadbare armor.
I grip the broom handle in both hands,
ready.

The sun is higher now in the eastern sky.
A horse and a sleigh
have been through recently.
I'm unsure where these tracks came from
or where they lead,
but I can tell someone's traveled in two
    directions,
has doubled back.

I stay with the sleigh tracks
until they turn north,
away from home.

I could follow,
try to catch up,
but I won't.
I'm going home.
It's dangerous,
but it's what I've chosen,
and I gather strength from knowing this.

I lift each boot
just to plunge it deep into the snow again,
a high-step march that hardly travels forward.
The broom handle is my cane.
My forehead burns.
My chemise, drenched with sweat,
is a frigid layer against my skin.
And no matter how much snow I suck,
my stomach isn't tricked.

Wolf,
show your face.
This would be an easy fight
for you.

When the sun is behind me,
I rest for a bit.
The quilt is both my shawl and cushion.

Even though I've traveled since just after
    daybreak,
I feel no closer
to my home.
And I can't possibly know
exactly where home is.

The quilt is soaked through,
but I'm not yet ready to start again.
The western horizon, both blue and white,
is so bright it's hard to look at long.
The only tracks I see are my own.

I rock for warmth,
pulling the quilt about me like a hood.

What if this is the end?
What if I've fought my way from that prison
   for nothing,
just to die out here?

Tears freeze to my eyelashes
as I stumble to my feet,
which are weighty as sacks of flour.
My legs are wet
from stockings to bloomers.

My shadow extends long before me.
If I'm not home soon,
I will not last the night.

Finally I turn,
face the western sky,
and watch the sun sink
lower,
lower.
It is gone.
I must move while there's still light.
I stamp my feet to rouse them.
Pain shoots through my toes,
a promise I'm still living.

I trudge toward the purple darkness
and turn sometimes to see if the sunlight
has taken pity on me,
if it might wait to see me home.
But it is well beyond that imaginary place
where the sky meets land—
the only light just a memory of this day.

Do I see or hear it first,
the shadow where the sun
once was,
distant bells,
the unsure step of a horse's hooves
battling the snow?

Someone is there!
I'm certain now.
I try to run,
trip on Mrs. Oblinger's quilt,
crash to the ground,
but I am up again.

"Hello! Hello!"
My voice is firm, like I've used it every day.
I flap my arms,
and the quilt unfurls.

Now the sleigh bells ring clearly.
"Over here!" I say.
A sleigh is steering toward me.
The horse slows,
then stops.

"May Betterly?"

"I'm May," I say,
and reach forward.
A firm hand grasps my wrist.

"Miss Betterly," the stranger says,
"are you all right?"

I've seen nothing move
for so long,
save grass pushing at my feet,
clouds,
rabbits,
this endless blowing snow.
And this is a person!
He settles me in his sleigh,
pulls a buffalo robe around me.

In the moonlight,
I make out the man's blue muffler,
a hat pushed low on his brow.
His eyes;
I have seen them before.

"I'm John Chapman," he says.
"I helped Mr. Oblinger with his floor."

The neighbor who brought the wood.

If Ma could see me,
she'd tell me to remember my manners.

"How do you do, Mr. Chapman?"

He nods to me.
"How do you do?"

I'm riding in a sleigh
away from the Oblingers' soddy!

We pass a clump of darkness,
some trees I counted last July?

"The storm came the first of December,"
    he says.
"I dug out last week,
drove into town.
That's when I heard . . ."
His eyes dart to me.
". . . heard the Oblingers were gone.

Seemed funny Oblinger would leave
without telling me.
I'd helped him some at his place.
He'd done some work on mine.
I asked if anyone knew where he was headed.
Heard all sorts of stories,
none of them the same:
his wife had run,
he'd given up and sold his land,
he would come back with family next spring."

Desperate to find the missus,
how easy it would be
to forget me.

Mr. Chapman turns.

"No one mentioned a girl.
I got to thinking,
if he'd run off like some folks said,
and with those wolves about,
what had become of you?"

Someone has thought of me.
These last few days,
someone *knew*.

"I came earlier this week to look for you,"
Mr. Chapman says.

"A couple of miles from my place,
something along the creek caught my eye.
I dug through the snow,
reached the spokes of a wheel.
Oblinger's wagon must have overturned,
slid over the edge of the ravine."

My heart claws at my throat,
remembering the way Mr. Oblinger raced.
Something *had* happened to him.
Mr. Oblinger never made it to town?
"Did you see—?"

Mr. Chapman shakes his head.
"I walked around,
looked for more."
He clears his throat.

The wolves.
There is nothing I can say.

"Rode faster then,

when I figured you were alone,
but the snow blew through again.
It was a wonder I made it home.

I dug myself out this morning.
Tried again at the Oblingers' this afternoon.
When I reached the soddy,
I found a hole,
some footprints,
and the house empty.
Followed those prints
until I found you."

"It was good of you, Mr. Chapman."
"Nothing more than any decent person
    would do."

The horse labors in the snow;
still, we're moving faster
than I ever did alone.
I lay my head back against the robe's soft fur.
I will see my family soon.

"My folks are just a few miles
southeast of town," I say.

His eyes are soft.
"It was foolish of you to try
to make it on your own.
Foolish,
and brave."

"Guess I'm the foolish type, then."

He laughs,
but not unkindly.

It is strange to hear this story:
a man I'd barely met
taking the time
to try to save me.

I ask, "Could you tell me the day?"

"It's Friday,
the fifteenth of December."

Pa delivered me
to the Oblingers
five months ago.

I listen but don't talk much;
there is too much to consider.

I am content to feel the wind
at my cheeks,
to take in the stars
scattered like marbles across the heavens,
to watch the horse's sturdy legs
step gingerly.

"Pa said he'd come just before Christmas,"
I hear myself saying.

Mr. Chapman says,
"I must have just beat him."

The air is sharp in my lungs.
I'm dizzied
from hunger,
or a lack of sleep,
or from the sweet strangeness
of my circumstance.

If I had waited just a few hours more,
Mr. Chapman would have found me
still buried beneath the snow.

But I didn't wait;
I pulled myself out of that place
and set to walking.
I left a trail for Mr. Chapman
to come to me.

Even though the world has looked
much the same
since Mr. Chapman stopped for me,
I know we're getting nearer.
The land feels familiar,
and then I see the gentle rise,
a wisp of smoke
escaping from the chimney.

"Stop!"
I shout,
then remember myself.
"Please stop."

Pa dug out,
as I'd imagined.
The land between the house and barn is clear.
I race toward the door
and shove it open.
"Ma,
Pa,
Hiram!"
I call.

Ma steps forward.

"May?"
Her confusion breaking into a smile.
"What are you doing here?"
I hug her,
not yet ready to explain.

Over her shoulder I see Mr. Chapman
at the barn,
talking to Pa.

Hiram rushes from the barn.
"May Betts!"
he yells,
his face lighting with a grin.
"What happened to your hair?"

Suddenly we're all together
between the barn and soddy.
Pa folds me in his arms.
"You were alone?"
he whispers.

I nod,
soaking in the warmth of his overcoat.

Ma's brought a mug of coffee
and a square of corn bread,
thick,
delicious.
The coffee burns
as I gulp it down.

"She's a strong girl,"
Mr. Chapman says.

Hiram's eyes meet mine.

"A girl who tries to cover fifteen miles
alone in the snow can handle just about
    anything."

Pa clears his throat and squeezes me.
Ma wraps her arms around the both of us.
I close my eyes,
lean on Pa's shoulder.

In time,
I'll tell about the wolf,
the empty apple barrel,
and the darkness.
For now,
I need no words.

Later,
after Mr. Chapman has bid us
good night,
Hiram holds out his hand.
"Come with me," he says.
He leads me to the rise where in the spring,
the wildflowers grow.
We stand together, side by side.

I don't know why sometimes
reading works for me,
but other times it doesn't.

I don't know why holding something
helps my words to form.

Maybe I'll never understand
exactly why I struggle.
I am
smart and capable
(as Miss Sanders used to say).

But
tonight in this stillness,
I realize there's no shame in hoping

for things that might seem out of reach.
I will take the teaching examination
when I'm old enough,
and if I fail,
I'll try again.

"You can keep your Christmas candy.
I don't want it anymore."
Hiram's eyes grow wide.
"You've seen it?"
I smile.
"Not yet,
but just you wait."

Even though I know
my geography,
even though I understand what is and
    isn't real,
there's no reason to stop hoping
that sometime
I might find it,
that distant place
where the sun journeys
and earth at last meets sky.

A Note from the Author

Growing up, I fell in love with the Little House books and talked about Laura Ingalls Wilder as if she were someone I knew personally. In the late nineteenth century, when Laura was a girl, schoolwork focused on recitation and memorization and favored students able to do those things well. When I became a teacher, I grew curious about what life must have been like for frontier children who found schooling a challenge. Would a girl who couldn't read well have been kept out of school? Would she have been chastised for not trying hard enough? Or would her intelligence have been recognized?

In this book, May struggles with dyslexia, a learning disability that hampers a person's capacity to process what is read. Dyslexia was unknown in the nineteenth century. It varies in each reader, although difficulties with reading fluency, word recognition, and comprehension are common, as are the omission of words and anxiety stemming from reading aloud. The techniques that prove helpful to May (repetition, reading in unison with one or more people, holding objects) have benefited many with dyslexia.

While *May B.* is a work of fiction, I've used the short-grass prairie of western Kansas as inspiration, imagining the Betterlys' and Oblingers' soddies in the outlying areas of Gove County. In the late 1870s, this part of Kansas was sparsely settled. Families homesteaded far from established towns, with neighbors miles away.

School terms typically ran summer and winter, allowing children to work during planting and harvest. Teachers were often young single women, as it was possible to receive a teaching certificate at fifteen or sixteen.

The text quoted in this book is from *The American Educational*

Reader, Number 5 (Ivison, Blakeman, Taylor, & Co., 1873), which I found in an antique shop just as I was starting to work on *May B*. I don't know if this book would have been available in Kansas schoolhouses at this time, though a similar reader would have been. Children often worked with the books accessible to them, many using in school the texts their families had brought from other parts of the country. I've included three lessons: "The Grandeur of the Sea" (author unknown), "A Hasty and Unjust Judgment," the passage about Mr. Goodman (attributed to "Aiken, adapted"), and "The Voice of the Wind" (author unknown). The last stanza of the poem is my own invention, something I altered to create more dramatic movement within the story.

For those interested in learning more about Kansas history, frontier living, or dyslexia, here are some helpful resources:

The Kansas Historical Society: kshs.org

The Prairie Museum of Art and History (Colby, Kansas): prairiemuseum.org

The International Dyslexia Association: interdys.org

Acknowledgments

Many thanks to those who have played a role in the creation of this book:

It's not often an author is lucky enough to write for two different editors. Nicole Geiger has been an unflagging enthusiast, careful reader, and mentor through this whole process. When she told me *May B.* was the sort of book she'd loved as a child, I knew it would be safe in her hands. Emily Seife's commitment to May and her personal growth pushed me to discover new ways to challenge my character and flesh her out more fully. Emily, I've appreciated every honest "not there yet" that has kept me working hard.

Michelle Humphrey, my agent, who found me in the slush and took a chance on my quiet verse novel. Your positive attitude and commitment as a colleague and friend have been invaluable.

Chris Griffin, of the Prairie Museum of Art and History in Colby, Kansas, for answering my questions about the landscape, plants, animals, insects, and waterways of western Kansas and for recommending reader and Kansas expert Ann Miner. Any inaccuracies that remain in the story are mine alone.

Shawn Goodman, fellow Elevensie author and literacy expert, for your insight into the frustrations and insecurities a dyslexic child experiences, as well as for sharing common reading challenges.

Ellen Ruffin and Abbie Woolridge of the de Grummond Children's Literature Collection and author Kate Bernheimer for answering my questions about Hansel and Gretel.

My parents, Milt and Polly, who made books a natural part of my upbringing; my grandparents, Dick and Gene, for exposing me to authors from Beatrix Potter to Wallace Stegner and for encouraging my imagination; and my sister, Chris, one of my biggest cheerleaders.

Dayle Arceneaux and Bonnie Rehage of the Bayou Readers' and Authors' Guild for encouraging me to continue this experiment in verse. My online critique partners, Denise Jaden, Weronika Janczuk, Elle Strauss, and Natalie Bahm, for your keen eyes. Natalie, I will be forever grateful for your question that led me to a newer, stronger ending.

Jamie Martin, for pointing me toward your antiques-shop find, the reader that played such a large part in the creation of this story, and for believing that this story had to be shared.

Molly Bolton and the rest of the Jambalaya Writers' Conference coordinators, for seeing promise in my story.

Dr. Jack Bedell of Southeastern Louisiana University, for including several early poems in *Louisiana Literature* magazine.

Cheryl Matherne, principal of St. Matthew's Episcopal School in Houma, Louisiana, for the beautiful way you supported my decision to devote myself to writing full-time, and for your love for this character.

C. S. Neal, for capturing perfectly with your artwork the atmosphere of the book. Your cover reminds me of beloved stories from my own childhood.

For the women who have gone before me: As Kansas historian Lilla Day Monroe said, "The world has never seen such hardihood, such perseverance, such devotion, nor such ingenuity in making the best of everything as was displayed by America's pioneer women. Their like has never been known" (Joanna Stratton, *Pioneer Women: Voices from the Kansas Frontier*, Touchstone, 1982, page 21).

My husband, Dan, and my boys, Noah and Caleb: it isn't easy living with someone who for years chases an impossible dream. Thank you for giving me the room and time to make a try at being a writer. And always, thank you for your love. You three mean the world to me.

And finally, my deepest gratitude to the One who binds up the brokenhearted and who extends dignity and compassion to the forgotten.

About the Author

Caroline Starr Rose was named a *Publishers Weekly* Flying Start Author for her debut novel, *May B.*, which was an ALA-ALSC Notable Children's Book and received two starred reviews.

Caroline spent her childhood in the deserts of Saudi Arabia and New Mexico, camping at the Red Sea in one and eating red chile in the other. As a girl, she danced ballet, raced through books by Laura Ingalls Wilder, and put on magic shows in a homemade cape. She has taught social studies and English, and worked to instill in her students a passion for books, an enthusiasm for experimenting with words, and a curiosity about the past. She lives in New Mexico. Visit her at carolinestarrrose.com.